OUR NICU Journey
9 WEEK DIARY

HOW TO USE THIS BOOK

Included in this journal are nine weeks of tracking prompts to record the progress of your precious little baby during their NICU stay. You can begin whenever you wish; there's no rules, please use this journal to suit your needs. Each day consists of two pages with prompts and plenty of room for journaling. To help you organize your thoughts and events, there's a line for the date and a place to enter your baby's NICU day. You can even color the cute little woodland animals.

Following every seven days, there is a place for entering additional information, adding photos, drawing or doodling. It will be rewarding to look back and remember their growth, daily activities, goals, struggles, and successes.

You will begin the journey by introducing your baby and sharing the events surrounding their entrance into the world. Next, there's a page dedicated to listing your visitors. On the last few pages, you can document the events of the long awaited day when you take your bundle of joy home.

Copyright 2019
Mellanie Kay Journals

Introducing

NAME

DATE OF BIRTH:

GESTATIONAL AGE:

TIME:

WEIGHT:

LENGTH:

HOSPITAL:

PROUD PARENTS:

MORE ABOUT MY BIRTHDAY:

Visitors

DATE | NAME

TODAY'S DATE: **NICU DAY #**

TODAY'S *Nurse*

TODAY'S *Doctor*

TODAY'S *Weather*

CURRENT *Events*

NOTES *& Reflections*

_____

_____

_____

_____

_____

_____

_____

_____

_____

_____

_____

_____

_____

_____

_____

_____

Positives

Hardships

Today... WE WERE BUSY!

FEEDING

READ

DIAPER

PHONE CALL

VIDEO CALL

ROCKED

SKIN ON SKIN

PRAYED

BATH

MASSAGE

TEMPERATURE

VISITORS

Today's STATS

WEIGHT:

LENGTH:

GESTATIONAL AGE:

LABS/MEDS:

PROCEDURES:

Feeding SCHEDULE

Milestones

Goals FOR TODAY

Questions TO ASK

TODAY'S DATE: NICU DAY #

TODAY'S *Nurse*

NOTES *& Reflections*

TODAY'S *Doctor*

TODAY'S *Weather*

CURRENT *Events*

Positives

Hardships

Today... WE WERE BUSY!

FEEDING

PHONE CALL

SKIN ON SKIN

MASSAGE

READ

VIDEO CALL

PRAYED

TEMPERATURE

DIAPER

ROCKED

BATH

VISITORS

Today's STATS

WEIGHT:

LENGTH:

GESTATIONAL AGE:

LABS/MEDS:

PROCEDURES:

Feeding SCHEDULE

Milestones

Questions TO ASK

Goals FOR TODAY

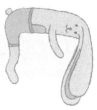

TODAY'S DATE: NICU DAY #

TODAY'S *Nurse*

NOTES *& Reflections*

_____
_____
_____

TODAY'S *Doctor*

_____
_____
_____

_____

TODAY'S *Weather*

_____
_____
_____

_____

CURRENT *Events*

_____
_____
_____

_____

Positives

Hardships

Today... WE WERE BUSY!

FEEDING

READ

DIAPER

PHONE CALL

VIDEO CALL

ROCKED

SKIN ON SKIN

PRAYED

BATH

MASSAGE

TEMPERATURE

VISITORS

Feeding SCHEDULE

_____   _____

_____   _____

_____   _____

_____   _____

Milestones

_____

_____

Questions TO ASK

Today's STATS

WEIGHT:

LENGTH:

GESTATIONAL AGE:

LABS/MEDS:

PROCEDURES:

Goals FOR TODAY

_____

_____

_____

_____

TODAY'S DATE:

TODAY'S *Nurse*

NOTES *& Reflections*

TODAY'S *Doctor*

TODAY'S *Weather*

CURRENT *Events*

Positives

Hardships

Today... WE WERE BUSY!

FEEDING   READ   DIAPER

PHONE CALL   VIDEO CALL   ROCKED

SKIN ON SKIN   PRAYED   BATH

MASSAGE   TEMPERATURE   VISITORS

Feeding SCHEDULE

Milestones

Questions TO ASK

Today's STATS

WEIGHT:

LENGTH:

GESTATIONAL AGE:

LABS/MEDS:

PROCEDURES:

Goals FOR TODAY

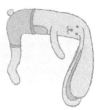

TODAY'S DATE: **NICU DAY #**

TODAY'S *Nurse*

TODAY'S *Doctor*

TODAY'S *Weather*

CURRENT *Events*

NOTES *& Reflections*

_____
_____
_____
_____
_____
_____
_____
_____
_____
_____
_____
_____
_____
_____

Positives

Hardships

Today... WE WERE BUSY!

FEEDING   READ   DIAPER

PHONE CALL   VIDEO CALL   ROCKED

SKIN ON SKIN   PRAYED   BATH

MASSAGE   TEMPERATURE   VISITORS

Feeding SCHEDULE

_____   _____

_____   _____

_____   _____

_____   _____

Milestones

_____

_____

Questions TO ASK

Today's STATS

WEIGHT:

LENGTH:

GESTATIONAL AGE:

LABS/MEDS:

PROCEDURES:

Goals FOR TODAY

_____

_____

_____

_____

TODAY'S DATE: **NICU DAY #**

TODAY'S *Nurse*   **NOTES** & *Reflections*

_____

_____

TODAY'S *Doctor*   _____

_____

_____

_____

TODAY'S *Weather*   _____

_____

_____

CURRENT *Events*   _____

_____

_____

Positives   *Hardships*

Today... WE WERE BUSY!

FEEDING	READ	DIAPER
PHONE CALL	VIDEO CALL	ROCKED
SKIN ON SKIN	PRAYED	BATH
MASSAGE	TEMPERATURE	VISITORS

Feeding SCHEDULE

_____   _____
_____   _____
_____   _____
_____   _____

Milestones

_____
_____

Questions TO ASK

Today's STATS

WEIGHT:

LENGTH:

GESTATIONAL AGE:

LABS/MEDS:

PROCEDURES:

Goals FOR TODAY

_____
_____
_____
_____

TODAY'S DATE: NICU DAY #

TODAY'S *Nurse*

NOTES *& Reflections*

TODAY'S *Doctor*

_____
_____
_____
_____
_____
_____

TODAY'S *Weather*

_____
_____
_____
_____

CURRENT *Events*

_____
_____
_____
_____

Positives   *Hardships*

Today... WE WERE BUSY!

FEEDING   READ   DIAPER

PHONE CALL   VIDEO CALL   ROCKED

SKIN ON SKIN   PRAYED   BATH

MASSAGE   TEMPERATURE   VISITORS

Feeding SCHEDULE

_____   _____

_____   _____

_____   _____

Milestones

_____

Today's STATS

WEIGHT:

LENGTH:

GESTATIONAL AGE:

LABS/MEDS:

PROCEDURES:

Questions TO ASK

Goals FOR TODAY

_____

_____

_____

_____

Photos

TODAY'S DATE: NICU DAY #

TODAY'S *Nurse*   **NOTES** *& Reflections*

_____

_____

TODAY'S *Doctor*   _____

_____

_____

_____

TODAY'S *Weather*   _____

_____

_____

_____

CURRENT *Events*   _____

_____

_____

Positives   *Hardships*

Today... WE WERE BUSY!

FEEDING

READ

DIAPER

PHONE CALL

VIDEO CALL

ROCKED

SKIN ON SKIN

PRAYED

BATH

MASSAGE

TEMPERATURE

VISITORS

Feeding SCHEDULE

_____

_____

_____

_____

_____

_____

Milestones

_____

Questions TO ASK

Today's STATS

WEIGHT:

LENGTH:

GESTATIONAL AGE:

LABS/MEDS:

PROCEDURES:

Goals FOR TODAY

_____

_____

_____

_____

TODAY'S DATE:

NICU DAY #

TODAY'S *Nurse*

TODAY'S *Doctor*

TODAY'S *Weather*

CURRENT *Events*

NOTES *& Reflections*

Positives

Hardships

Today... WE WERE BUSY!

FEEDING

READ

DIAPER

PHONE CALL

VIDEO CALL

ROCKED

SKIN ON SKIN

PRAYED

BATH

MASSAGE

TEMPERATURE

VISITORS

Feeding SCHEDULE

Milestones

Questions TO ASK

Today's STATS

WEIGHT:

LENGTH:

GESTATIONAL AGE:

LABS/MEDS:

PROCEDURES:

Goals FOR TODAY

TODAY'S DATE: NICU DAY #

TODAY'S *Nurse*

NOTES *& Reflections*

TODAY'S *Doctor*

TODAY'S *Weather*

CURRENT *Events*

Positives

Hardships

Today... WE WERE BUSY!

FEEDING   READ   DIAPER

PHONE CALL   VIDEO CALL   ROCKED

SKIN ON SKIN   PRAYED   BATH

MASSAGE   TEMPERATURE   VISITORS

Feeding SCHEDULE

_____   _____

_____   _____

_____   _____

_____   _____

Milestones

_____

_____

Questions TO ASK

Today's STATS

WEIGHT:

LENGTH:

GESTATIONAL AGE:

LABS/MEDS:

PROCEDURES:

Goals FOR TODAY

_____

_____

_____

_____

TODAY'S DATE: NICU DAY #

TODAY'S *Nurse*

NOTES *& Reflections*

TODAY'S *Doctor*

TODAY'S *Weather*

CURRENT *Events*

Positives

Hardships

Today... WE WERE BUSY!

FEEDING	READ	DIAPER
PHONE CALL	VIDEO CALL	ROCKED
SKIN ON SKIN	PRAYED	BATH
MASSAGE	TEMPERATURE	VISITORS

Feeding SCHEDULE

Milestones

Questions TO ASK

Today's STATS

WEIGHT:

LENGTH:

GESTATIONAL AGE:

LABS/MEDS:

PROCEDURES:

Goals FOR TODAY

TODAY'S DATE: NICU DAY #

TODAY'S *Nurse*

TODAY'S *Doctor*

TODAY'S *Weather*

CURRENT *Events*

NOTES *& Reflections*

_____
_____
_____
_____
_____
_____
_____
_____
_____
_____
_____
_____
_____
_____

Positives

Hardships

Today... WE WERE BUSY!

FEEDING   READ   DIAPER

PHONE CALL   VIDEO CALL   ROCKED

SKIN ON SKIN   PRAYED   BATH

MASSAGE   TEMPERATURE   VISITORS

Feeding SCHEDULE

Milestones

Questions TO ASK

Today's STATS

WEIGHT:

LENGTH:

GESTATIONAL AGE:

LABS/MEDS:

PROCEDURES:

Goals FOR TODAY

TODAY'S DATE:

NICU DAY #

TODAY'S *Nurse*

NOTES *& Reflections*

TODAY'S *Doctor*

TODAY'S *Weather*

CURRENT *Events*

Positives

Hardships

Today... WE WERE BUSY!

FEEDING ___   READ ___   DIAPER ___

PHONE CALL ___   VIDEO CALL ___   ROCKED ___

SKIN ON SKIN ___   PRAYED ___   BATH ___

MASSAGE ___   TEMPERATURE ___   VISITORS ___

___

Feeding SCHEDULE

_____   _____

_____   _____

_____   _____

_____   _____

Milestones

_____

_____

Questions TO ASK

Today's STATS

WEIGHT:

LENGTH:

GESTATIONAL AGE:

LABS/MEDS:

PROCEDURES:

Goals FOR TODAY

_____

_____

_____

_____

TODAY'S DATE:

NICU DAY #

TODAY'S *Nurse*

NOTES *& Reflections*

TODAY'S *Doctor*

TODAY'S *Weather*

CURRENT *Events*

Positives

Hardships

Today... WE WERE BUSY!

FEEDING	READ	DIAPER
PHONE CALL	VIDEO CALL	ROCKED
SKIN ON SKIN	PRAYED	BATH
MASSAGE	TEMPERATURE	VISITORS

Feeding SCHEDULE

Milestones

Questions TO ASK

Today's STATS

WEIGHT:

LENGTH:

GESTATIONAL AGE:

LABS/MEDS:

PROCEDURES:

Goals FOR TODAY

Photos

TODAY'S DATE:

NICU DAY #

TODAY'S *Nurse*

NOTES & *Reflections*

_____
_____
_____
_____
_____
_____

TODAY'S *Doctor*

_____
_____
_____
_____
_____

TODAY'S *Weather*

_____
_____
_____
_____

CURRENT *Events*

_____
_____
_____
_____

Positives

Hardships

Today... WE WERE BUSY!

FEEDING   READ   DIAPER

PHONE CALL   VIDEO CALL   ROCKED

SKIN ON SKIN   PRAYED   BATH

MASSAGE   TEMPERATURE   VISITORS

Feeding SCHEDULE

_____   _____

_____   _____

_____   _____

Milestones

_____

Questions TO ASK

Today's STATS

WEIGHT:

LENGTH:

GESTATIONAL AGE:

LABS/MEDS:

PROCEDURES:

Goals FOR TODAY

TODAY'S DATE:

NICU DAY #

TODAY'S *Nurse*

TODAY'S *Doctor*

TODAY'S *Weather*

CURRENT *Events*

NOTES *& Reflections*

_____
_____
_____
_____
_____
_____
_____
_____
_____
_____
_____
_____
_____
_____
_____

Positives

Hardships

Today... WE WERE BUSY!

FEEDING   READ   DIAPER

PHONE CALL   VIDEO CALL   ROCKED

SKIN ON SKIN   PRAYED   BATH

MASSAGE   TEMPERATURE   VISITORS

Today's STATS

WEIGHT:

LENGTH:

GESTATIONAL AGE:

LABS/MEDS:

PROCEDURES:

Feeding SCHEDULE

Milestones

Questions TO ASK

Goals FOR TODAY

TODAY'S DATE:　　　　　　　**NICU DAY #**

TODAY'S *Nurse*

NOTES *& Reflections*

TODAY'S *Doctor*

TODAY'S *Weather*

CURRENT *Events*

Positives

Hardships

Today... WE WERE BUSY!

FEEDING   READ   DIAPER

PHONE CALL   VIDEO CALL   ROCKED

SKIN ON SKIN   PRAYED   BATH

MASSAGE   TEMPERATURE   VISITORS

Feeding SCHEDULE

Milestones

Questions TO ASK

Today's STATS

WEIGHT:

LENGTH:

GESTATIONAL AGE:

LABS/MEDS:

PROCEDURES:

Goals FOR TODAY

TODAY'S DATE: NICU DAY #

TODAY'S *Nurse*

NOTES *& Reflections*

_____
_____
_____
_____
_____

TODAY'S *Doctor*

_____
_____
_____
_____
_____

TODAY'S *Weather*

_____
_____
_____
_____

CURRENT *Events*

_____
_____
_____
_____

Positives

Hardships

Today... WE WERE BUSY!

- FEEDING
- PHONE CALL
- SKIN ON SKIN
- MASSAGE

- READ
- VIDEO CALL
- PRAYED
- TEMPERATURE

- DIAPER
- ROCKED
- BATH
- VISITORS

Feeding SCHEDULE

_____ _____

_____ _____

_____ _____

_____ _____

Milestones

_____

_____

Questions TO ASK

Today's STATS

WEIGHT:

LENGTH:

GESTATIONAL AGE:

LABS/MEDS:

PROCEDURES:

Goals FOR TODAY

_____

_____

_____

_____

TODAY'S DATE:

NICU DAY #

TODAY'S *Nurse*

NOTES *& Reflections*

_____
_____
_____
_____
_____
_____
_____

TODAY'S *Doctor*

TODAY'S *Weather*

_____
_____
_____
_____
_____

CURRENT *Events*

_____
_____
_____

Positives

Hardships

Today... WE WERE BUSY!

FEEDING   READ   DIAPER

PHONE CALL   VIDEO CALL   ROCKED

SKIN ON SKIN   PRAYED   BATH

MASSAGE   TEMPERATURE   VISITORS

Feeding SCHEDULE

Milestones

Questions TO ASK

Today's STATS

WEIGHT:

LENGTH:

GESTATIONAL AGE:

LABS/MEDS:

PROCEDURES:

Goals FOR TODAY

TODAY'S DATE: **NICU DAY #**

TODAY'S *Nurse*

NOTES *& Reflections*

TODAY'S *Doctor*

TODAY'S *Weather*

CURRENT *Events*

Positives

Hardships

Today... WE WERE BUSY!

FEEDING   READ   DIAPER

PHONE CALL   VIDEO CALL   ROCKED

SKIN ON SKIN   PRAYED   BATH

MASSAGE   TEMPERATURE   VISITORS

Feeding SCHEDULE

Milestones

Questions TO ASK

Today's STATS

WEIGHT:

LENGTH:

GESTATIONAL AGE:

LABS/MEDS:

PROCEDURES:

Goals FOR TODAY

TODAY'S DATE: NICU DAY #

TODAY'S *Nurse*

TODAY'S *Doctor*

TODAY'S *Weather*

CURRENT *Events*

NOTES & *Reflections*

_____
_____
_____
_____
_____
_____
_____
_____
_____
_____
_____
_____
_____

Positives

Hardships

Today... WE WERE BUSY!

FEEDING   READ   DIAPER

PHONE CALL   VIDEO CALL   ROCKED

SKIN ON SKIN   PRAYED   BATH

MASSAGE   TEMPERATURE   VISITORS

Feeding SCHEDULE

Milestones

Questions TO ASK

Today's STATS

WEIGHT:

LENGTH:

GESTATIONAL AGE:

LABS/MEDS:

PROCEDURES:

Goals FOR TODAY

Photos

TODAY'S DATE:

TODAY'S *Nurse*

NOTES *& Reflections*

TODAY'S *Doctor*

TODAY'S *Weather*

CURRENT *Events*

Positives

Hardships

Today... WE WERE BUSY!

FEEDING   READ   DIAPER

PHONE CALL   VIDEO CALL   ROCKED

SKIN ON SKIN   PRAYED   BATH

MASSAGE   TEMPERATURE VISITORS

Feeding SCHEDULE

Milestones

Questions TO ASK

Today's STATS

WEIGHT:

LENGTH:

GESTATIONAL AGE:

LABS/MEDS:

PROCEDURES:

Goals FOR TODAY

TODAY'S DATE:

NICU DAY #

TODAY'S *Nurse*

NOTES & *Reflections*

TODAY'S *Doctor*

TODAY'S *Weather*

CURRENT *Events*

Positives

Hardships

Today... WE WERE BUSY!

FEEDING   READ   DIAPER

PHONE CALL   VIDEO CALL   ROCKED

SKIN ON SKIN   PRAYED   BATH

MASSAGE   TEMPERATURE   VISITORS

Feeding SCHEDULE

Milestones

Questions TO ASK

Today's STATS

WEIGHT:

LENGTH:

GESTATIONAL AGE:

LABS/MEDS:

PROCEDURES:

Goals FOR TODAY

TODAY'S DATE:

NICU DAY #

TODAY'S *Nurse*

NOTES *& Reflections*

TODAY'S *Doctor*

TODAY'S *Weather*

CURRENT *Events*

Positives

Hardships

Today... WE WERE BUSY!

FEEDING   READ   DIAPER

PHONE CALL   VIDEO CALL   ROCKED

SKIN ON SKIN   PRAYED   BATH

MASSAGE   TEMPERATURE   VISITORS

Feeding SCHEDULE

Milestones

Questions TO ASK

Today's STATS

WEIGHT:

LENGTH:

GESTATIONAL AGE:

LABS/MEDS:

PROCEDURES:

Goals FOR TODAY

TODAY'S DATE: NICU DAY #

TODAY'S *Nurse*

TODAY'S *Doctor*

TODAY'S *Weather*

CURRENT *Events*

NOTES & *Reflections*

_____

_____

_____

_____

_____

_____

_____

_____

_____

_____

_____

_____

_____

_____

_____

Positives

Hardships

Today... WE WERE BUSY!

FEEDING   READ   DIAPER

PHONE CALL   VIDEO CALL   ROCKED

SKIN ON SKIN   PRAYED   BATH

MASSAGE   TEMPERATURE   VISITORS

Feeding SCHEDULE

Milestones

Questions TO ASK

Today's STATS

WEIGHT:

LENGTH:

GESTATIONAL AGE:

LABS/MEDS:

PROCEDURES:

Goals FOR TODAY

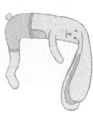

TODAY'S DATE:

NICU DAY #

TODAY'S *Nurse*

NOTES *& Reflections*

TODAY'S *Doctor*

TODAY'S *Weather*

CURRENT *Events*

Positives

Hardships

Today... WE WERE BUSY!

FEEDING   READ   DIAPER

PHONE CALL   VIDEO CALL   ROCKED

SKIN ON SKIN   PRAYED   BATH

MASSAGE   TEMPERATURE   VISITORS

Feeding SCHEDULE

Milestones

Questions TO ASK

Today's STATS

WEIGHT:

LENGTH:

GESTATIONAL AGE:

LABS/MEDS:

PROCEDURES:

Goals FOR TODAY

TODAY'S DATE: NICU DAY #

TODAY'S *Nurse*

NOTES & *Reflections*

TODAY'S *Doctor*

_____

_____

_____

_____

TODAY'S *Weather*

_____

_____

_____

_____

_____

_____

CURRENT *Events*

_____

_____

_____

_____

Positives

Hardships

Today... WE WERE BUSY!

FEEDING READ DIAPER

PHONE CALL VIDEO CALL ROCKED

SKIN ON SKIN PRAYED BATH

MASSAGE TEMPERATURE VISITORS

Feeding SCHEDULE

Milestones

Questions TO ASK

Today's STATS

WEIGHT:

LENGTH:

GESTATIONAL AGE:

LABS/MEDS:

PROCEDURES:

Goals FOR TODAY

TODAY'S DATE: **NICU DAY #**

TODAY'S *Nurse*

NOTES *& Reflections*

_____
_____
_____
_____
_____
_____

TODAY'S *Doctor*

_____
_____
_____
_____
_____

TODAY'S *Weather*

_____
_____
_____
_____
_____

CURRENT *Events*

_____
_____
_____
_____
_____

Positives

Hardships

Today... WE WERE BUSY!

FEEDING   READ   DIAPER

PHONE CALL   VIDEO CALL   ROCKED

SKIN ON SKIN   PRAYED   BATH

MASSAGE   TEMPERATURE   VISITORS

Feeding SCHEDULE

Milestones

Questions TO ASK

Today's STATS

WEIGHT:

LENGTH:

GESTATIONAL AGE:

LABS/MEDS:

PROCEDURES:

Goals FOR TODAY

Photos

TODAY'S DATE: NICU DAY #

TODAY'S *Nurse*

TODAY'S *Doctor*

TODAY'S *Weather*

CURRENT *Events*

NOTES & *Reflections*

_____
_____
_____
_____
_____
_____
_____
_____
_____
_____
_____
_____
_____
_____

Positives

Hardships

Today... WE WERE BUSY!

FEEDING   READ   DIAPER

PHONE CALL   VIDEO CALL   ROCKED

SKIN ON SKIN   PRAYED   BATH

MASSAGE   TEMPERATURE   VISITORS

Feeding SCHEDULE

_____   _____

_____   _____

_____   _____

Milestones

_____

_____

Questions TO ASK

Today's STATS

WEIGHT:

LENGTH:

GESTATIONAL AGE:

LABS/MEDS:

PROCEDURES:

Goals FOR TODAY

_____

_____

_____

_____

TODAY'S DATE:

NICU DAY #

TODAY'S *Nurse*

NOTES & *Reflections*

TODAY'S *Doctor*

TODAY'S *Weather*

CURRENT *Events*

_____
_____
_____
_____
_____
_____
_____
_____
_____
_____
_____
_____
_____

Positives

Hardships

Today... WE WERE BUSY!

FEEDING   READ   DIAPER

PHONE CALL   VIDEO CALL   ROCKED

SKIN ON SKIN   PRAYED   BATH

MASSAGE   TEMPERATURE   VISITORS

Feeding SCHEDULE

_____   _____

_____   _____

_____   _____

_____   _____

Milestones

_____

_____

Questions TO ASK

Today's STATS

WEIGHT:

LENGTH:

GESTATIONAL AGE:

LABS/MEDS:

PROCEDURES:

Goals FOR TODAY

_____

_____

_____

_____

TODAY'S DATE: **NICU DAY #**

TODAY'S *Nurse*

TODAY'S *Doctor*

TODAY'S *Weather*

CURRENT *Events*

NOTES *& Reflections*

_____
_____
_____
_____
_____
_____
_____
_____
_____
_____
_____
_____
_____
_____

Positives

Hardships

Today... WE WERE BUSY!

FEEDING   READ   DIAPER

PHONE CALL   VIDEO CALL   ROCKED

SKIN ON SKIN   PRAYED   BATH

MASSAGE   TEMPERATURE   VISITORS

Feeding SCHEDULE

Milestones

Questions TO ASK

Today's STATS

WEIGHT:

LENGTH:

GESTATIONAL AGE:

LABS/MEDS:

PROCEDURES:

Goals FOR TODAY

TODAY'S DATE: NICU DAY #

TODAY'S *Nurse*

TODAY'S *Doctor*

TODAY'S *Weather*

CURRENT *Events*

NOTES *& Reflections*

_____
_____
_____
_____
_____
_____
_____
_____
_____
_____
_____
_____
_____
_____
_____

Positives

Hardships

Today... WE WERE BUSY!

FEEDING ___

PHONE CALL ___

SKIN ON SKIN ___

MASSAGE ___

READ ___

VIDEO CALL ___

PRAYED ___

TEMPERATURE ___

DIAPER ___

ROCKED ___

BATH ___

VISITORS ___

___

Feeding SCHEDULE

_____

_____

_____

_____

_____

_____

Milestones

_____

_____

Questions TO ASK

Today's STATS

WEIGHT:

LENGTH:

GESTATIONAL AGE:

LABS/MEDS:

PROCEDURES:

Goals FOR TODAY

_____

_____

_____

_____

_____

TODAY'S DATE: NICU DAY #

TODAY'S *Nurse*   **NOTES** *& Reflections*

_____
_____
_____
TODAY'S *Doctor*   _____
_____
_____
_____
TODAY'S *Weather*   _____
_____
_____
_____
_____
CURRENT *Events*   _____
_____
_____
_____

Positives   *Hardships*

Today... WE WERE BUSY!

FEEDING   READ   DIAPER

PHONE CALL   VIDEO CALL   ROCKED

SKIN ON SKIN   PRAYED   BATH

MASSAGE   TEMPERATURE   VISITORS

Feeding SCHEDULE

Milestones

Questions TO ASK

Today's STATS

WEIGHT:

LENGTH:

GESTATIONAL AGE:

LABS/MEDS:

PROCEDURES:

Goals FOR TODAY

TODAY'S DATE: NICU DAY #

TODAY'S *Nurse*

NOTES & *Reflections*

TODAY'S *Doctor*

TODAY'S *Weather*

CURRENT *Events*

Positives

Hardships

Today... WE WERE BUSY!

FEEDING   READ   DIAPER

PHONE CALL   VIDEO CALL   ROCKED

SKIN ON SKIN   PRAYED   BATH

MASSAGE   TEMPERATURE   VISITORS

Today's STATS

WEIGHT:

LENGTH:

GESTATIONAL AGE:

LABS/MEDS:

PROCEDURES:

Feeding SCHEDULE

Milestones

Questions TO ASK

Goals FOR TODAY

TODAY'S DATE:

NICU DAY #

TODAY'S *Nurse*

TODAY'S *Doctor*

TODAY'S *Weather*

CURRENT *Events*

NOTES *& Reflections*

Positives

Hardships

Today... WE WERE BUSY!

FEEDING   READ   DIAPER

PHONE CALL   VIDEO CALL   ROCKED

SKIN ON SKIN   PRAYED   BATH

MASSAGE   TEMPERATURE VISITORS

Today's STATS

WEIGHT:

LENGTH:

GESTATIONAL AGE:

LABS/MEDS:

PROCEDURES:

Feeding SCHEDULE

Milestones

Questions TO ASK

Goals FOR TODAY

Photos

TODAY'S DATE:

NICU DAY #

TODAY'S *Nurse*

NOTES *& Reflections*

TODAY'S *Doctor*

TODAY'S *Weather*

CURRENT *Events*

Positives

Hardships

Today... WE WERE BUSY!

FEEDING   READ   DIAPER

PHONE CALL   VIDEO CALL   ROCKED

SKIN ON SKIN   PRAYED   BATH

MASSAGE   TEMPERATURE   VISITORS

Feeding SCHEDULE

Milestones

Questions TO ASK

Today's STATS

WEIGHT:

LENGTH:

GESTATIONAL AGE:

LABS/MEDS:

PROCEDURES:

Goals FOR TODAY

TODAY'S DATE:

NICU DAY #

TODAY'S *Nurse*

NOTES *& Reflections*

TODAY'S *Doctor*

TODAY'S *Weather*

CURRENT *Events*

Positives

Hardships

Today... WE WERE BUSY!

FEEDING   READ   DIAPER

PHONE CALL   VIDEO CALL   ROCKED

SKIN ON SKIN   PRAYED   BATH

MASSAGE   TEMPERATURE   VISITORS

Feeding SCHEDULE

Milestones

Questions TO ASK

Today's STATS

WEIGHT:

LENGTH:

GESTATIONAL AGE:

LABS/MEDS:

PROCEDURES:

Goals FOR TODAY

TODAY'S *Nurse*

TODAY'S *Doctor*

TODAY'S *Weather*

CURRENT *Events*

NOTES & *Reflections*

Positives

Hardships

Today... WE WERE BUSY!

FEEDING   READ   DIAPER

PHONE CALL   VIDEO CALL   ROCKED

SKIN ON SKIN   PRAYED   BATH

MASSAGE   TEMPERATURE   VISITORS

Today's STATS

WEIGHT:

LENGTH:

GESTATIONAL AGE:

LABS/MEDS:

PROCEDURES:

Feeding SCHEDULE

Milestones

Questions TO ASK

Goals FOR TODAY

TODAY'S DATE: **NICU DAY #**

TODAY'S *Nurse*

NOTES & *Reflections*

_____

TODAY'S *Doctor*

_____

_____

_____

_____

TODAY'S *Weather*

_____

_____

_____

_____

CURRENT *Events*

_____

_____

_____

_____

Positives

Hardships

Today... WE WERE BUSY!

FEEDING   READ   DIAPER

PHONE CALL   VIDEO CALL   ROCKED

SKIN ON SKIN   PRAYED   BATH

MASSAGE   TEMPERATURE   VISITORS

Feeding SCHEDULE

_____   _____

_____   _____

_____   _____

_____   _____

Milestones

_____

_____

Questions TO ASK

Today's STATS

WEIGHT:

LENGTH:

GESTATIONAL AGE:

LABS/MEDS:

PROCEDURES:

Goals FOR TODAY

_____

_____

_____

_____

_____

TODAY'S DATE:

NICU DAY #

TODAY'S *Nurse*

NOTES *& Reflections*

TODAY'S *Doctor*

TODAY'S *Weather*

CURRENT *Events*

Positives

Hardships

Today... WE WERE BUSY!

FEEDING   READ   DIAPER

PHONE CALL   VIDEO CALL   ROCKED

SKIN ON SKIN   PRAYED   BATH

MASSAGE   TEMPERATURE   VISITORS

Feeding SCHEDULE

Milestones

Questions TO ASK

Today's STATS

WEIGHT:

LENGTH:

GESTATIONAL AGE:

LABS/MEDS:

PROCEDURES:

Goals FOR TODAY

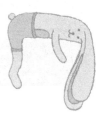

TODAY'S DATE:

NICU DAY #

TODAY'S *Nurse*

TODAY'S *Doctor*

TODAY'S *Weather*

CURRENT *Events*

NOTES & *Reflections*

_____
_____
_____
_____
_____
_____
_____
_____
_____
_____
_____
_____
_____
_____
_____
_____

Positives

Hardships

Today... WE WERE BUSY!

FEEDING   READ   DIAPER

PHONE CALL   VIDEO CALL   ROCKED

SKIN ON SKIN   PRAYED   BATH

MASSAGE   TEMPERATURE   VISITORS

Feeding SCHEDULE

_____   _____
_____   _____
_____   _____
_____   _____

Milestones

_____
_____

Questions TO ASK

Today's STATS

WEIGHT:

LENGTH:

GESTATIONAL AGE:

LABS/MEDS:

PROCEDURES:

Goals FOR TODAY

_____
_____
_____
_____

TODAY'S DATE:

NICU DAY #

TODAY'S *Nurse*

NOTES *& Reflections*

TODAY'S *Doctor*

TODAY'S *Weather*

CURRENT *Events*

Positives

Hardships

Today... WE WERE BUSY!

FEEDING   READ   DIAPER

PHONE CALL   VIDEO CALL   ROCKED

SKIN ON SKIN   PRAYED   BATH

MASSAGE   TEMPERATURE   VISITORS

Today's STATS

WEIGHT:

LENGTH:

GESTATIONAL AGE:

LABS/MEDS:

PROCEDURES:

Feeding SCHEDULE

Milestones

Questions TO ASK

Goals FOR TODAY

Photos

_____

_____

_____

_____

_____

_____

_____

_____

_____

TODAY'S DATE:

NICU DAY #

TODAY'S *Nurse*

NOTES *& Reflections*

TODAY'S *Doctor*

TODAY'S *Weather*

CURRENT *Events*

Positives

Hardships

Today... WE WERE BUSY!

FEEDING   READ   DIAPER

PHONE CALL   VIDEO CALL   ROCKED

SKIN ON SKIN   PRAYED   BATH

MASSAGE   TEMPERATURE   VISITORS

Feeding SCHEDULE

Milestones

Questions TO ASK

Today's STATS

WEIGHT:

LENGTH:

GESTATIONAL AGE:

LABS/MEDS:

PROCEDURES:

Goals FOR TODAY

TODAY'S DATE: NICU DAY #

TODAY'S *Nurse*

NOTES & *Reflections*

TODAY'S *Doctor*

TODAY'S *Weather*

CURRENT *Events*

Positives

Hardships

Today... WE WERE BUSY!

FEEDING   READ   DIAPER

PHONE CALL   VIDEO CALL   ROCKED

SKIN ON SKIN   PRAYED   BATH

MASSAGE   TEMPERATURE   VISITORS

Feeding SCHEDULE

_____   _____
_____   _____
_____   _____
_____   _____

Milestones

_____
_____

Questions TO ASK

Today's STATS

WEIGHT:

LENGTH:

GESTATIONAL AGE:

LABS/MEDS:

PROCEDURES:

Goals FOR TODAY

_____
_____
_____
_____
_____

TODAY'S DATE:

NICU DAY #

TODAY'S *Nurse*

NOTES & *Reflections*

TODAY'S *Doctor*

TODAY'S *Weather*

CURRENT *Events*

Positives

Hardships

Today... **WE WERE BUSY!**

FEEDING   READ   DIAPER

PHONE CALL   VIDEO CALL   ROCKED

SKIN ON SKIN   PRAYED   BATH

MASSAGE   TEMPERATURE   VISITORS

Feeding **SCHEDULE**

_____   _____

_____   _____

_____   _____

_____   _____

Milestones

_____

_____

Questions **TO ASK**

Today's **STATS**

WEIGHT:

LENGTH:

GESTATIONAL AGE:

LABS/MEDS:

PROCEDURES:

Goals **FOR TODAY**

_____

_____

_____

_____

TODAY'S DATE:

NICU DAY #

TODAY'S *Nurse*

NOTES & *Reflections*

TODAY'S *Doctor*

TODAY'S *Weather*

CURRENT *Events*

Positives

Hardships

Today... WE WERE BUSY!

FEEDING

READ

DIAPER

PHONE CALL

VIDEO CALL

ROCKED

SKIN ON SKIN

PRAYED

BATH

MASSAGE

TEMPERATURE

VISITORS

Today's STATS

WEIGHT:

LENGTH:

GESTATIONAL AGE:

LABS/MEDS:

PROCEDURES:

Feeding SCHEDULE

Milestones

Questions TO ASK

Goals FOR TODAY

TODAY'S DATE:

NICU DAY #

TODAY'S *Nurse*

NOTES & *Reflections*

TODAY'S *Doctor*

TODAY'S *Weather*

CURRENT *Events*

Positives

Hardships

Today... WE WERE BUSY!

FEEDING	READ	DIAPER
PHONE CALL	VIDEO CALL	ROCKED
SKIN ON SKIN	PRAYED	BATH
MASSAGE	TEMPERATURE	VISITORS

Feeding SCHEDULE

Milestones

Questions TO ASK

Today's STATS

WEIGHT:

LENGTH:

GESTATIONAL AGE:

LABS/MEDS:

PROCEDURES:

Goals FOR TODAY

TODAY'S DATE:

NICU DAY #

TODAY'S *Nurse*

NOTES *& Reflections*

TODAY'S *Doctor*

_____
_____
_____
_____
_____

TODAY'S *Weather*

_____
_____
_____
_____

CURRENT *Events*

_____
_____
_____
_____

Positives

Hardships

Today... WE WERE BUSY!

FEEDING   READ   DIAPER

PHONE CALL   VIDEO CALL   ROCKED

SKIN ON SKIN   PRAYED   BATH

MASSAGE   TEMPERATURE   VISITORS

Feeding SCHEDULE

Milestones

Questions TO ASK

Today's STATS

WEIGHT:

LENGTH:

GESTATIONAL AGE:

LABS/MEDS:

PROCEDURES:

Goals FOR TODAY

TODAY'S DATE:

NICU DAY #

TODAY'S *Nurse*

TODAY'S *Doctor*

TODAY'S *Weather*

CURRENT *Events*

NOTES & *Reflections*

Positives

Hardships

Today... WE WERE BUSY!

FEEDING   READ   DIAPER

PHONE CALL   VIDEO CALL   ROCKED

SKIN ON SKIN   PRAYED   BATH

MASSAGE   TEMPERATURE   VISITORS

Feeding SCHEDULE

_____   _____
_____   _____
_____   _____
_____   _____

Milestones

_____
_____

Questions TO ASK

Today's STATS

WEIGHT:

LENGTH:

GESTATIONAL AGE:

LABS/MEDS:

PROCEDURES:

Goals FOR TODAY

_____
_____
_____
_____

Photos

_____

_____

_____

_____

_____

_____

_____

_____

_____

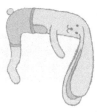

TODAY'S DATE:

NICU DAY #

TODAY'S *Nurse*

NOTES *& Reflections*

TODAY'S *Doctor*

_____

_____

_____

_____

_____

TODAY'S *Weather*

_____

_____

_____

_____

_____

CURRENT *Events*

_____

_____

_____

_____

Positives

Hardships

Today... WE WERE BUSY!

FEEDING   READ   DIAPER

PHONE CALL   VIDEO CALL   ROCKED

SKIN ON SKIN   PRAYED   BATH

MASSAGE   TEMPERATURE   VISITORS

Feeding SCHEDULE

Milestones

Questions TO ASK

Today's STATS

WEIGHT:

LENGTH:

GESTATIONAL AGE:

LABS/MEDS:

PROCEDURES:

Goals FOR TODAY

TODAY'S DATE:

NICU DAY #

TODAY'S *Nurse*

NOTES & *Reflections*

TODAY'S *Doctor*

_____
_____
_____
_____
_____
_____

TODAY'S *Weather*

_____
_____
_____
_____
_____

CURRENT *Events*

_____
_____
_____
_____

Positives

Hardships

Today... WE WERE BUSY!

FEEDING   READ   DIAPER

PHONE CALL   VIDEO CALL   ROCKED

SKIN ON SKIN   PRAYED   BATH

MASSAGE   TEMPERATURE   VISITORS

Feeding SCHEDULE

Milestones

Questions TO ASK

Today's STATS

WEIGHT:

LENGTH:

GESTATIONAL AGE:

LABS/MEDS:

PROCEDURES:

Goals FOR TODAY

TODAY'S DATE: **NICU DAY #**

TODAY'S *Nurse*

TODAY'S *Doctor*

TODAY'S *Weather*

CURRENT *Events*

NOTES & *Reflections*

_____

_____

_____

_____

_____

_____

_____

_____

_____

_____

_____

_____

_____

_____

Positives

Hardships

Today... WE WERE BUSY!

FEEDING　　　READ　　　DIAPER

PHONE CALL　　VIDEO CALL　　ROCKED

SKIN ON SKIN　　PRAYED　　BATH

MASSAGE　　TEMPERATURE　　VISITORS

Feeding SCHEDULE

Milestones

Questions TO ASK

Today's STATS

WEIGHT:

LENGTH:

GESTATIONAL AGE:

LABS/MEDS:

PROCEDURES:

Goals FOR TODAY

TODAY'S DATE: NICU DAY #

TODAY'S *Nurse*

NOTES & *Reflections*

TODAY'S *Doctor*

TODAY'S *Weather*

CURRENT *Events*

Positives

Hardships

Today... WE WERE BUSY!

FEEDING   READ   DIAPER

PHONE CALL   VIDEO CALL   ROCKED

SKIN ON SKIN   PRAYED   BATH

MASSAGE   TEMPERATURE   VISITORS

Feeding SCHEDULE

Milestones

Questions TO ASK

Today's STATS

WEIGHT:

LENGTH:

GESTATIONAL AGE:

LABS/MEDS:

PROCEDURES:

Goals FOR TODAY

TODAY'S DATE: **NICU DAY #**

TODAY'S *Nurse*

TODAY'S *Doctor*

TODAY'S *Weather*

CURRENT *Events*

NOTES & *Reflections*

_____

_____

_____

_____

_____

_____

_____

_____

_____

_____

_____

_____

_____

Positives

Hardships

Today... WE WERE BUSY!

FEEDING   READ   DIAPER

PHONE CALL   VIDEO CALL   ROCKED

SKIN ON SKIN   PRAYED   BATH

MASSAGE   TEMPERATURE   VISITORS

Feeding SCHEDULE

_____   _____

_____   _____

_____   _____

_____   _____

Milestones

_____

_____

Questions TO ASK

Today's STATS

WEIGHT:

LENGTH:

GESTATIONAL AGE:

LABS/MEDS:

PROCEDURES:

Goals FOR TODAY

_____

_____

_____

_____

_____

TODAY'S DATE: **NICU DAY #**

TODAY'S *Nurse*

NOTES *& Reflections*

TODAY'S *Doctor*

TODAY'S *Weather*

CURRENT *Events*

Positives

Hardships

Today... WE WERE BUSY!

FEEDING   READ   DIAPER

PHONE CALL   VIDEO CALL   ROCKED

SKIN ON SKIN   PRAYED   BATH

MASSAGE   TEMPERATURE   VISITORS

Today's STATS

WEIGHT:

LENGTH:

GESTATIONAL AGE:

LABS/MEDS:

PROCEDURES:

Feeding SCHEDULE

Milestones

Questions TO ASK

Goals FOR TODAY

TODAY'S DATE: **NICU DAY #**

TODAY'S *Nurse*

NOTES & *Reflections*

TODAY'S *Doctor*

TODAY'S *Weather*

CURRENT *Events*

Positives

Hardships

Today... WE WERE BUSY!

FEEDING   READ   DIAPER

PHONE CALL   VIDEO CALL   ROCKED

SKIN ON SKIN   PRAYED   BATH

MASSAGE   TEMPERATURE   VISITORS

Feeding SCHEDULE

Milestones

Questions TO ASK

Today's STATS

WEIGHT:

LENGTH:

GESTATIONAL AGE:

LABS/MEDS:

PROCEDURES:

Goals FOR TODAY

Photos

TODAY'S DATE:

NICU DAY #

TODAY'S *Nurse*

TODAY'S *Doctor*

TODAY'S *Weather*

CURRENT *Events*

NOTES *& Reflections*

Positives

Hardships

Today... WE WERE BUSY!

FEEDING   READ   DIAPER

PHONE CALL   VIDEO CALL   ROCKED

SKIN ON SKIN   PRAYED   BATH

MASSAGE   TEMPERATURE   VISITORS

Feeding SCHEDULE

Milestones

Questions TO ASK

Today's STATS

WEIGHT:

LENGTH:

GESTATIONAL AGE:

LABS/MEDS:

PROCEDURES:

Goals FOR TODAY

TODAY'S DATE: **NICU DAY #**

TODAY'S *Nurse*

NOTES & *Reflections*

TODAY'S *Doctor*

TODAY'S *Weather*

CURRENT *Events*

Positives

Hardships

Today... WE WERE BUSY!

FEEDING   READ   DIAPER

PHONE CALL   VIDEO CALL   ROCKED

SKIN ON SKIN   PRAYED   BATH

MASSAGE   TEMPERATURE   VISITORS

Today's STATS

WEIGHT:

LENGTH:

GESTATIONAL AGE:

LABS/MEDS:

PROCEDURES:

Feeding SCHEDULE

Milestones

Questions TO ASK

Goals FOR TODAY

TODAY'S *Nurse*

NOTES & *Reflections*

TODAY'S *Doctor*

_____
_____
_____
_____
_____
_____

TODAY'S *Weather*

_____
_____
_____
_____
_____

CURRENT *Events*

_____
_____
_____

Positives

Hardships

Today... WE WERE BUSY!

FEEDING

PHONE CALL

SKIN ON SKIN

MASSAGE

READ

VIDEO CALL

PRAYED

TEMPERATURE

DIAPER

ROCKED

BATH

VISITORS

Feeding SCHEDULE

Milestones

Questions TO ASK

Today's STATS

WEIGHT:

LENGTH:

GESTATIONAL AGE:

LABS/MEDS:

PROCEDURES:

Goals FOR TODAY

TODAY'S DATE:

NICU DAY #

TODAY'S *Nurse*

NOTES *& Reflections*

TODAY'S *Doctor*

TODAY'S *Weather*

CURRENT *Events*

Positives

Hardships

Today... WE WERE BUSY!

FEEDING   READ   DIAPER

PHONE CALL   VIDEO CALL   ROCKED

SKIN ON SKIN   PRAYED   BATH

MASSAGE   TEMPERATURE   VISITORS

Feeding SCHEDULE

_____   _____

_____   _____

_____   _____

Milestones

_____

_____

Questions TO ASK

Today's STATS

WEIGHT:

LENGTH:

GESTATIONAL AGE:

LABS/MEDS:

PROCEDURES:

Goals FOR TODAY

_____

_____

_____

_____

_____

TODAY'S DATE: **NICU DAY #**

TODAY'S *Nurse*

TODAY'S *Doctor*

TODAY'S *Weather*

CURRENT *Events*

NOTES *& Reflections*

Positives

Hardships

Today... WE WERE BUSY!

FEEDING   READ   DIAPER

PHONE CALL   VIDEO CALL   ROCKED

SKIN ON SKIN   PRAYED   BATH

MASSAGE   TEMPERATURE   VISITORS

Feeding SCHEDULE

Milestones

Questions TO ASK

Today's STATS

WEIGHT:

LENGTH:

GESTATIONAL AGE:

LABS/MEDS:

PROCEDURES:

Goals FOR TODAY

TODAY'S DATE: **NICU DAY #**

TODAY'S *Nurse*

NOTES *& Reflections*

TODAY'S *Doctor*

TODAY'S *Weather*

CURRENT *Events*

Positives

Hardships

Today... WE WERE BUSY!

FEEDING   READ   DIAPER

PHONE CALL   VIDEO CALL   ROCKED

SKIN ON SKIN   PRAYED   BATH

MASSAGE   TEMPERATURE   VISITORS

Today's STATS

WEIGHT:

LENGTH:

GESTATIONAL AGE:

LABS/MEDS:

PROCEDURES:

Feeding SCHEDULE

Milestones

Questions TO ASK

Goals FOR TODAY

TODAY'S DATE:

NICU DAY #

TODAY'S *Nurse*

TODAY'S *Doctor*

TODAY'S *Weather*

CURRENT *Events*

NOTES & *Reflections*

_____
_____
_____
_____
_____
_____
_____
_____
_____
_____
_____
_____
_____
_____

Positives

Hardships

Today... WE WERE BUSY!

FEEDING   READ   DIAPER

PHONE CALL   VIDEO CALL   ROCKED

SKIN ON SKIN   PRAYED   BATH

MASSAGE   TEMPERATURE   VISITORS

Feeding SCHEDULE

Milestones

Questions TO ASK

Today's STATS

WEIGHT:

LENGTH:

GESTATIONAL AGE:

LABS/MEDS:

PROCEDURES:

Goals FOR TODAY

Photos

_____

_____

_____

_____

_____

_____

_____

_____

_____

Going Home

DATE:

GESTATIONAL AGE:

WEIGHT & LENGTH:

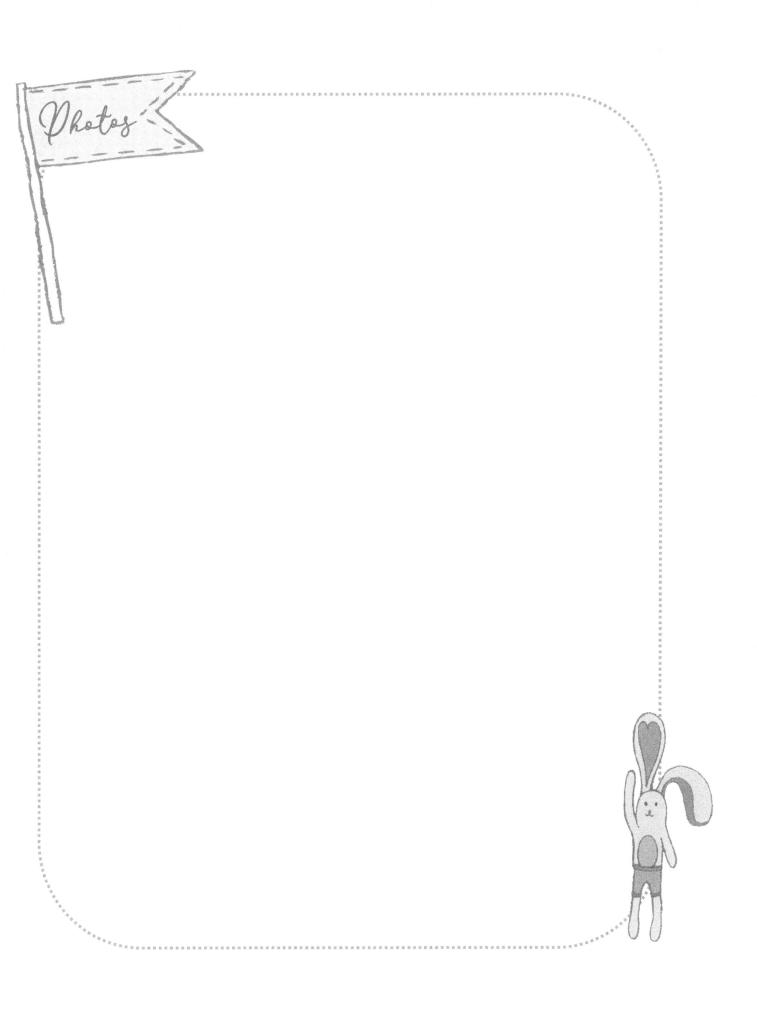

Photos